To:

# The Mailbox of the Kindred Spirit

## LB SEDLACEK

2-15-20

Thank you for being here! Hope you get to visit the real Mailbox!

L. B. Sedlacek

"The Mailbox of the Kindred Spirit"
By LB Sedlacek

**Second Edition**

# From the Author:

This chapbook is about the Kindred Spirit mailbox on Sunset Beach, NC (technically Bird Island). It's about 2 miles from the Sunset Beach pier.

I discovered it by accident. I was looking online for something educational involved reading for us to do on our beach trip to the NC coast and I stumbled across it.

It isn't easy to find, even though it is right on the beach. We had to ask several people where it was as we walked along. We considered giving up many times, but ultimately decided to keep going and finally we did get there.

It was almost dark when we arrived and completely dark when we left. We did have flashlights and our little feisty dog with us. It was quite a trudge in the dark back to the pier. But along the way we saw all kinds of sand crabs which were fun to see. We saw ships night fishing with their bright lights out in the ocean. We saw the blinking lights of the pier guiding us back.

Had we not kept going, we never would've experienced these things. And did I mention the glorious sunset we saw on the way there?

It's in one of the pictures in the book. It was definitely a spiritual experience for us. It's certainly worth a visit if you are ever that way! *~LB Sedlacek*

# A Thank You From the Author

The author wishes to thank the following people for supporting this project and poetry on Kickstarter – here's wishing you poetical success!

## A Special Thank You to:
**Doris Bush**
**Greysmoke**
**Raymond Mullikin**
**Toby Rush**
**Jimmy Tan San Tek**
**Jim Wright**
**and the other Kickstarter supporters of this project**

## Without You This Project Would Not Have Been Possible!
*~LB Sedlacek*

# TABLE OF CONTENTS

## The Beginning:  Sunset Beach Pier

It took some time to find it across the sound across the bridge, the highways, the drives, then back across again and up and down 40th street the end of the beach where there's little public parking only a few spaces but it's the best place to watch the sun go down still I drove up and down each street of Sunset Beach finally parking at the pier and going inside to pay my $8 I ask where the mailbox is and the guy tells me it's about 2 miles away and that it's almost dark I'll never make it but I tell him I'm going anyway and so he tells me I don't have to pay to park and he points out the window up the beach and tells me to go that way and to take a flashlight and I do and I had read about the mailbox on the internet even before you told me about it before you wrote to me and I read about a flag that would mark the spot but there was no flag only people walking back the other way laughing at me when I'd say that I was going to the mailbox telling me it was a long way away and to look for the brown sign with nothing on it and that would mark the way it would be near there and to keep going to the end of the sand dunes line.

# The Middle:  The Story

**Chapter One**

"Hey Ernie!  Ernie!"

I look up, stand, swipe my hands through my hair, thick, white, curly, out of control.  "Yeah?  What?"  I am gruff.  I yell.  I know I'm gruff.  I'm 58 years old.  Why would I not be?  I've been single all my life.  Lived alone all my life.  Worked at the Golf Club all my life.  First as a cook in the little grill downstairs, then a Caddy.  Then in the Pro Shop behind the counter.  Then as a Salesman at the Pro Shop.  Then back behind the counter.  Then a Caddy.  Then the Head Cook at the little grill.  Then as a Cook at the upstairs restaurant.  Back to Caddy again.  Then a Golf Pro.  A real golf pro with tips and some extra extra benefits if you know what I mean.  Then I became Assistant Manager.  Then Manager.

The Rionel Golf Club had fallen on hard times peaking in the 60's and 70's, continuing forth in the 80's and 90's, holding on through the 2000's but then towards the latter half the 2010's on not so much.  People don't play golf as much.  Deals aren't made on golf courses like they used to be.  Golf courses, even private ones, tend to be public to get enough money in to keep them running.  I was still the Manager, but I was about to be retired.

RGC wanted someone younger, hipper, cheaper to take my place and bring in social media. Social media and golf? Yeah, maybe you'd post a picture of yourself playing golf, but would that bring in more players? Really?

I stare at the younger hipper cheaper woman RGC had brought in to take my place. She stands there, skinny, tall, long brown hair, and she grins at me.

I don't smile back. I just bark "What is it now?"

"Ernie." She drawls it out and smiles. "There's some boxes in the storage shed I need you to take a look at and see what's in there. Whatever you don't think we should keep, it's gonna be tossed. Or you can have it. You know as a souvenir of this place." She smiles again and holds her hands up and out likes she's a waiter holding a tray.

We are standing in the upstairs restaurant. It's after lunch and before dinner so the long L shaped room is empty. The gold carpets had just been vacuumed by the cleaning staff. The tables wiped down and set up for dinner by the wait staff.

RCG served all three meals in the snack bar downstairs and only lunch and dinner in the upstairs restaurant. It was a small club in an L shaped wooden building with two floors. The upstairs was the restaurant with a corner divided off like a lounge with a couple of sofas and a big screen TV. The downstairs had the snack bar and the Pro Shop.

I point down the stairs besides the kitchen. "Fine. I'll head down and take a look. Let you know what I found tomorrow."

She smiles yet again and crosses her arms. "Why thank you, Ernie. That's mighty kind of you."

I cross my arms and grin back at her. "Why you are quite welcome."

I had been told her name numerous times. I had chosen to forget it. This young thin thing with no experience at a golf club ever whose Daddy had gotten her the job was the one taking my place. She was taking RGC away from me.

**Chapter Two**

I used to be able to climb the stairs two at a time and go down them three at a time. I was holding the rail. I was going down one stair at a time. I was not stopping to look at the black and white photographs hanging on both sides of the dingy yellow walls. The photos were of past players. None of them were well-known except in our tiny small North Carolina mountain town community.

A big deal in a small place, but a no big deal in a large city. Sure we had wealthy golfers, and wealthy people in the town but a question of how much wealth and how far it would go somewhere else or even in a big city was quite a big question. I was trained to treat everyone the same except out on the course where the big tippers and the constant players got the best tee times, the best caddies, the best of all RGC had to offer.

RCG was only a golf club with the Pro Shop, the formal dining restaurant and the snack bar. The snack bar also was a bar serving liquor and beers. There was a variety of mixed drinks and domestic or imported beers to sample.

Many of our members would come to the snack bar for supper and then stay half the night sitting around the bar playing cards. There wasn't always a lot of golf playing at the golf club.

We held classes for the player's kids. It was a cheap and easy way to cultivate a new set of players. But with all the online stuff golfing at RCG had lost some of its appeal. Miss Young Thing was supposed to bring all that back and bring in the younger generation.

No one seemed to notice or mind when she smiled her big smile nodding her chin up and down above the big gap in her showing cleavage and said she had never played golf and had no interest in learning. She wasn't married. She said she didn't know anyone that played golf, not even her parents or grandparents.

I was old enough to be her grandfather, that much I knew. I would work out my last days. I would earn my severance pay which amounted to a couple of months. No benefits. I would lose those on my last day. I would lose my free membership to RGC, too. That much I wouldn't mind. I didn't intend to come back to play golf or to visit or to drink, play cards, shop in the Pro Shop or anything else.

I wasn't going to stop playing golf. I would keep playing. There were plenty of courses I could still play, slow moving or not.

## Chapter Three

I hit the last stair and was in the side room off the bar.  The snack bar was to the left.  The bar to the right.  Plenty of round wooden tables dotted the room.  The walls were covered in more black and white pictures hanging off of plywood walls.  The carpet was a dingy yellow mustard color with a few spots bleached white from where the clean up crew had to get up throw up once in a while.  Most of the members weren't boozers and knew when to stop, but sometimes a guest would have one too many.

The wine ususaly caused some trouble.  We didn't have too many wine drinkers.  Once in a while someone would want one or they'd bring a girl to learn to play golf or a wife to check out where they were hanging out all night and then order a glass of wine.  The wine was sometimes so old it had turned to vinegar, but it was hard to tell until someone drank it or drank too much of it.

I step over the stained wine spots in the carpet to the back hall that led to the kitchen.  I duck through the door and stepped into a wide white room full of metal cabinets and sinks.  A pile of dishes soaked in ceiling high suds in the corner.  I look down to see if the floor had been hosed off yet.

The kitchen was the only place with a tiled floor.  The floor was brick red and concave towards the middle so after the floors were washed the water would pour down the drain in the middle.

The kitchen floor was dry. I sniff the air, and smelled rolls and some other kind of bread cooking. A couple of pots bubbled on the stove. Must be soup and sandwich day, I think. I always like soup and sandwich day.

My tummy grumbled and I skipped the urge to taste a sample of the boiling soup. I push on out the back door and turn to the small locked closet hidden underneath the first floor overhang, under the stairs, just off the kitchen door. It was padlocked. I was the only one with a key, but I knew soon that would change.

## Chapter Four

The storage room was about as wide and long as an average cellar except it wasn't underground. I stood back and let the damp stale air rush past me. I knew keeping the door open wouldn't help the smell or the air. I thought about heading to the maintenance area underneath the clubhouse. It's possible they'd have an extra face mask I could have.

I pinch my nose and grab the flashlight hanging from a long nail just inside the door. I flip it on and scan the faint light up and down the rectangular space. I sigh. It's already been cleaned out.

Miss cheap and fabulous was right about only boxes being left. I shake my head and back up a few steps. I shut off the flashlight.

I grip the flashlight tight in my hand. It's the same flashlight I left in the storage shed so many years ago. I planned to keep it. Let Miss fabulous get a new one, I think.

A few steps later me and my reclaimed flashlight are at the maintenance area. It's too early for anyone to be working back here yet.

Maintenance was set up underneath the club house. The two floor club house was built up on stilts so that the golf carts and a few VIP's could park underneath it. It kept the carts dry and out of the elements.

I push past some parked carts. Some there for storage, some needing work done, some just extra and parked there to be out of the way.

Shoved up against a pole, behind the last row of stored carts is what I'm after. A dolly. Another one of my contributions to the Club. I didn't think I could sneak it, though, under my shirt or in my pocket to take it home. I could tell Miss Fabulous it was mine, but I knew she wouldn't believe me, not without a receipt.

I grumble at the thought of her taking over and doing away with traditions all her new fangled ideas as I pull the dolly behind me back to the shed. It was worth the trip. All the boxes, all three of them stack real nice on the silver dolly.

I relock the storage shed without the flashlight. I tuck it into my pants pocket. I grab the dolly and haul it behind me.

I pull it into the snack bar and park it beside a round wooden table sitting right at the stairwell. I pull the boxes off and set them under the table. I push the dolly against the wall.

For a moment, I stand and look at the boxes. They aren't labled. I'm not sure where to start. I glance over at the bar. I decide that's where I should start.

I help myself to a domestic beer. I don't care what brand it is, just that it's cold. The tiny refrigerator hums underneath the bar.

There hadn't been money to renovate it, so it looked almost the same as when I'd started working there. The wooden bar top was the same. The same rectangle mirrors covered the walls behind the bar.

The stools had been replaced with ones covered in a faux red burgundy and black leather of some kind. They hadn't cracked or peeled so we never saw the need to replace them.

Miss Young Thing, though, I had heard was going to knock out the bar and get rid of beer, wine, liquor and replace all of it with healthy drinks. She was going to stock energy drinks, vegetable and fruit drinks, smoothies, and varieties of bottled water. The Snack Bar would have a new menu too. No more burgers, fries, onion rings, milkshakes, sundaes, fried pickles, eggs, bacon, or livermush sandwiches. Nope! It would all be healthy stuff, too. Wraps and salads. Veggies and dips. Fresh fruits. Goodbye baked goods! Goodbye chips!

I grab a snack bag from behind the counter of the Snack Bar. A missing beer, a missing bag of pretzels won't matter to her since she was going to toss it all out anyway. The tossing of the RGC traditions would commence a few hours from now as soon as I walked out the door for the last time.

I roll my eyes and scratch my chin. The photos that had been on the walls these years, she'll get rid of those too, I think. She was going to replace everything. I might as well enjoy the last hours I had left.

I pull back a chair, open my bags of pretzels, twist open my beer and sit down. I jerk off the lid to the first box. It was full of mildewed newspapers. I wasn't even going to try and sift through those.

"Toss," I mutter.

The second box had broken trophies and medals in it, probably left from an old golf tournament. I mutter "toss" again.

The third box, ah the third box. The box I should've started with, the box I'd always wondered about, the box with what I had thought about off and on for years but told myself after high school that summer and then after graduating college and coming back to think of no more. There they were, though, just like you'd said the last time I saw you at RCG. There they were. Just like you told me.

And I didn't believe you. Why didn't I believe you?

# The Middle:  The Letters

**Chapter Five**

*Letter One*

Dear Ernie:

I had fun with you today at the golf course. It was fun to use the putter and putt the golf balls. I didn't know you could do that indoors. I hope you like your summer job. I may get a summer job, too. My Mom thinks she can get me one at the Snack Bar so maybe I'll see you around. My Mom made me write you this thank you note. I hope you like it.

Sincerely,

Your friend Melody

*Letter Two*

Dear Ernie:

Night golf? Who knew. I was a little worried on prom night riding around in the golf cart on the course at night, but it was fun. My Mom says you are a good guy. She sees how you treat the club members when she's cooking up food in the Snack Bar. Says you are always polite. That's why she let you take me to my prom.

Sometimes I wish we went to the same high school, but with us living on opposite ends of the county, me in the west part, you in the east part I guess there's no way for that to happen unless one of us moves. But we can always meet at the golf course.

I did enjoy summer camp. We made crafts, swam in the ocean, went horseback riding, learned to fish. I can catch a fish now, but I'm not going to gut it!

Maybe I would've liked working at the Snack Bar but my Mom says she wants me to have more opportunity than she did growing up in the same small southern mountain town. That's why she sent me to stay with my Grandparents on the coast and to camp. You would've liked the beach. It's called Sunset. The sunsets really are pretty here.

Sincerely,

Melody

*Letter Three*

Dear Ernie:

It doesn't look like I'll be back to the golf course anytime soon. My parents think it's best for me to concentrate on my studies. Did I tell you I'm attending an all girls college? I'm taking courses in biology and chemistry and the basic ones like english and math courses, too.

I was so excited you won a scholarship at the county graduation party. We didn't get much time to visit because there were so many people, but we had such a fun time dancing. My favorite part was taking a walk with you outside.

Were your parents excited that you won the scholarship?

I miss RGC. It's different here. Everyone says they have trouble understanding my southern mountain lilt of an accent whatever that means.

Will you be going to college? Will you please write to me? I think of you often and the prom. You were such a gentleman.

Maybe you could visit me here?

With love,

Melody

*Letter Four*

Dear Ernie:

I heard you graduated with a business degree from the College and that you are still working at RGC. My Mom thinks they will be making you the Assistant Manager soon. I bet one day you will be running the whole place. Do you ever think you will leave it or leave the area?

I have two more years to go. I'm one of the few girls to ever study biology, but the boys have gotten used to me. The girls have accepted it too. At least my friends have and that's all that matters.

My mom calls me once a week. She never writes. I enjoy writing. I sit in the library when the campus is quiet and read or write letters.

She said you asked if I would be home for the summer. I thought I might be, but if I am it will be only to drop off things, clothes and pick up new clothes my mom has sewn for me. She has really gotten good at sewing from patterns. All the girls rave about my dresses. Can you imagine me climbing around in a swamp or river wearing wading boots and a dress?

Did I tell you, I'm learning to fish? The boys in my biology classes take turns showing me what to do. I do love seafood. It's fresh and tasty here.

A couple of the boys have Dads who can get them good summer jobs in biology or ecology. They think they can help me too. Fingers crossed.

Please write to me sometime and tell me how you are doing and what it's been like working at RGC all this time.

See you soon I hope,

Melody

*Letter Five*

Dear Ernie:

I'm graduating! Can you believe it? I am one of the first women to graduate with a degree in environmental science. My parents and grandparents are so proud. I wish you could've come to my graduation. I guess you had other things going on. My mom says you are doing well at RGC. It seems I always miss you when I'm in town, at least that what my mom says.

I have my first job interview! I'm going to be interviewing for a job at one of the local science museums. I have another interview lined up at one of our state aquariums. I would be most happy to have either job, I think.

Even though I am right on the beach here at Sunset Beach, I don't spend that much time on it at least not during the day. I like to walk the beach at sunset or later. I take a flashlight and my grandfather's dog, Fiasco (yes, that's really his name!), and we go hunting for sand crabs. Sometimes, we look for seashells.

I sell the crabs or seashells for spending money. Maybe with my new job I won't have to go beach combing anymore!

I have learned to fish off the piers. It's different than fishing in a stream or river or lake or even off of a boat!

Once in a great while, I even catch something!

I hope you'll write me this time – if you don't want to write a letter you could get a card or even call.  My mom will give you the number, I'm sure.

Okay, Ernie.  I hope you're well.


Yours always,

Melody

*Letter Six*

Ernie:

How long has it been? I've been at my full time job in Ocean Isle for almost three years now. We've endured all sorts of weather. I'm used to it now, I suppose.

My Grandparents left me the little beach house on Sunset. The commute is so long. Okay, not really. Some days it may take me 15 minutes if there's a lot of traffic.

My Mom says they've made you Manager now of RGC. Congratulations! Are you still playing golf, are you still a golf pro or have you given all that up?

I bet you're wondering if I've met anyone? Yes, I have. They are all fisherman! They took me in and taught me how to fish. I love frying up a batch straight from the ocean. The taste is incredible.

It's quiet here. I spend most days at the museum. I still walk the beach at Sunset. On weekends, I fish! My fishermen friends say that makes me liberated, whatever that means.

Hope you are doing well.

Yours,

Melody

*Letter Seven*

Ernie:


Hey Ernie!  Where have the years taken us?  I guess it's been awhile since I wrote you.  I did get your cards.  Thank you.  My Grandparents lived a full life.  They left me the house.  I will miss them both.

How's your job going?  It's really something that you became the Manager.  I wish I knew more about what you've been up to all these years. I would've liked to see you, too.

One time, I started to call you but my Grandfather said that wasn't proper.  I don't know why I listened to him!  I'm sure he meant well.

My Mom said you had a girl anyway and that maybe the two of you would marry.  Maybe you did.  Maybe you have a whole passel of children to keep you busy.

I didn't marry.  I did go out with a few fellas here and there.  But none of them like the water as much as me.  I do have my fishermen buddies.  We spend much time on the pier.

You should see the sunsets here, the soft orange and purple and red glow.  The sunrises are a hot orange and yellow.  It makes getting up worthwhile every day.

I still work at the museum.  I'm sure I will retire there.

I'm not much for writing letters anymore, but I still like to fish off the Ocean Isle pier and take long walks on Sunset Beach.  There's a mailbox there too.  Near the end of the beach, the coast line, maybe two miles from the pier.  If you're ever in the area, you should check it out.  I'll leave something there for you.


Yours always,

Melody

*Letters Eight and Nine (Type written on Note Cards):*

Ernie:

I hope this finds you well. My handwriting is getting too shaky now to write much. I still fish, though.

I bet you are wondering about this mailbox I told you about in my last letter. Go to Sunset Beach. Park at the pier. Bring good walking shoes and your dog if you have one.

It's two miles south approximately. Start walking!

The mailbox is almost beyond the end of the sand dunes line. There's a small flagpole there, but I can't promise it will stay with the weather.

There's a bench, too. Come on. Sit a spell. Read the mail.

Yours truly,

Melody

Ernie:


I had to send you one more card.  It's hard to type much on an index card.  You can find me on the pier at Ocean Isle.  If you ever get to the coast, look for me.


Again yours,

Melody

# The Middle:  The Flashbacks

## Chapter Six

"Hey Ernie! Ernie!"

I look up. Pull down my visor. Push it up again on my head. A young woman with darkish blonde hair rushed towards me.

"Ernie!"

She jumps up and wraps her arms around me. I jump back, and pull her hands from my neck.

"Miss? I'm afraid you must have me confused with someone else. It happened a lot. I'm Ernie. I'm the Manager."

The young woman giggles. She tugs on her shorts. Puts her hair up into a pony tail.

"Oh silly. Has it been that long? You don't remember me? C'mon, think about it."

I stare at her face, oval and a little tan. I look into her emerald green eyes. I'm a little taller than her, but not by much. She's slender. She talks with a lilting southern accent that echoes more South Carolina than North Carolina.

I mutter "Melody?"

She nods. She cries. She hugs me again.

## Chapter Seven

We sat out by the back 9.  It was out of the way a bit from the rest of the course.  Under some shade trees.  Secluded from the highways bordering the field.

"So that's it.  You're the Manager.  You're the PGA Professional.  That's all it took?"

I sighed and tried not to look into her shimmering green gem eyes.  "It was at one of our club tournaments.  You know we have those.  The Gold Tee Slam, Senior Slam, Dog Fight, All Play Slam."  I sighed.  Took off my sunglasses.  My face, arms, and legs were golden brown from the sun.  My scalp was more red because I'd just had my hair cut into a crew cut.  "It was at the Couples Event.  I had no one to play with so-."

She smacks my arm and giggles.  "Didn't you get any of my letters?  Didn't you read them?  You could've invited me!"

"Melody, I don't know--."

She shakes her head.  "I figured you didn't answer because you'd gotten older, lost your hair, gotten fat, lost your teeth, or you'd gotten in trouble with the law or something.  I never figured on a--."  She stares at the ground.  Wipes her eyes.  "I never figured on another girl!"

"I'm sorry, Melody.  I didn't get your letters."  I stand up, stand behind her and put my arms around her.  "I figured you were a college girl, a college grad, living on the coast somewhere – that much I did know about you – and that you'd moved on and should've moved on.  Why stay hooked up with a guy that collects Cart and Green fees for a living?  RCG was built in the 1920's.  Even though it was designed by Donald Ross it's a membership run golf course.  We maintain the course well, but it's public golf in our little community.  I'm never going to amount to what you deserve anyway.  Your mom pretty much implied that, she'd never answer my questions about you anyway so I figured you'd moved on, you'd done better than me."

She shakes me off, pushes my arms away, shoves me back away from her. "Oh Ernie.  You are a fool!"

# The Middle:  Return to Present Day

**Chapter Eight**

I dump the contents of one of the boxes out on the table. I take the empty box and toss the letters inside heading on to my desk, my soon to be former desk. Miss Young Thing stands by and watches as I clear my personals from the office that will now be here. After I'm done and stare at the half full box and think that my life at RGC had been reduced to a few photos, pens, and golf awards, nothing much more.

She giggles, puts her hands on her hips. "Guess it's all mine now, Ernie."

I cringe at the way she says my name in her clipped up northern accent. "Guess so."

I push past her and go on out the door not stopping, not saying goodbye to anyone. There's no one left really who I want to stay in touch with. It's all new people. It's all a membership run facility now and the members had spoken saying that me and my salary needed to go.

Go, I would. But where?

I sit in my pick-up truck and think about where to go for about five minutes. I'd spent so much time, day and night, at the club that I didn't really know what to do with free time.

I finally shift into gear and head for the library. Several minutes after that, I'm reading about Sunset Beach and Ocean Isle, the best ways to get there and what to do once you're there.  I have a stack of six books on a small desk in the back of the main room near the Biographies.  No one's ever in the back near the Biographies, I'd always heard.

After I get halfway through one of the books, someone does come back to the Biographies section.  It's the Librarian, an old friend from High School.  She smiles and brings me some paper and a pencil.  She whispers "Not everything has to be done on a computer, you know."

**Chapter Nine**

I stand and stare at my Jeep. It's all packed up with everything I own. My home, my apartment building for the last thirty something years is full of neighbors I no longer know. I to them, was Ernie the old guy in apartment #11.

Miss Young Thing had my last paycheck mailed to me. She told me before I left that it might be upsetting to the members if I came by to pick it up. She'd also discouraged me from playing at the RGC or even coming over as a guest player. Way to do business, I thought, not that my not being there would stop anyone I knew from playing there if they wanted to.

I ran my hands over the tees in my pocket. My very first ones. I remembered showing Melody how to use a tee, how to use the automatic putter to practice inside at the pro shop. I smiled thinking of her wondering if she'd ever learned to play golf.

I take one last look at the building. The yellow paint had faded to an off white. The bricks were cracked. The roof sagged. It was affordable housing that I'd needed when I first started out. As I went along I never saw a reason to upgrade to purchase anything. My needs had been simple. Money for transportation, food, clothing, a place to sleep at night and golf.

Golfing at the beach is the way golf is meant to be. That's what someone at RGC used to say. I could no longer remember if it was a member, or an employee, or maybe some kind of quote that had been hanging on the wall until Miss Young Thing came aboard.

I rented a room for a week at a small ocean front hotel in Ocean Isle. It was right on the beach. It was close enough to off season, fall would soon be here and so I had the room cheap for the week with an option to renew another week.

The room was small. It had a dresser, a TV, a high round table with two chairs, a bed, a closet area with an ironing board, a desk, a wet bar with a mini fridge, and a microwave and coffee maker on a small rectangle table. It was much like my old apartment except none of the furniture was mine.

I sink into the bed and flip through the local paper and some local brochures. The drive had been quick, less than five hours. I only stopped for gas and a bathroom break at the same time on the way.

I couldn't believe how many years it had taken me to get to the beach, to Melody's Ocean Isle. I couldn't believe how close it had been, how close she had been all this time.

# Chapter Ten

My first sunrise on the beach, I spend on the balcony. I watch the thick orange glow rise up over the palm trees. The sky lights up yellow and orange.

The ocean's gentle roar is the only noise. There are no other sounds.

I sip from the cup of hotel room coffee I made with in the complementary coffee maker. It is weak, watery, but still coffee.

The ocean breeze cools it off quick enough. Even so, I finish every last drop.

I take my time showering, dressing in a light button down Hawaiian shirt, and shorts – something I hadn't worn in years. I stand at the wet bar and comb my hair. It was thick, a little curly, but all gray and wavy. I needed it cut. I'd always kept it trimmed, but I didn't see the need now for a smart looking haircut.

I tidy up my toiletries. Empty my suitcase of shirts, socks, underwear, shorts, pants, and a couple of sweatshirts and jackets into the dresser drawers. I stuff my suitcase behind the ironing board in the corner of the closet area. I knew I would not be using that. I had never learned to iron.

The mini fridge was across from the ironing board. I open it and look inside. It was cold, but empty. There would be room enough, though, for any groceries I might want in the room.

The thought of groceries puts eating breakfast first on my agenda. The hotel came with a free breakfast buffet. I grab my key card and head down the breezeway.

I go through four doors and four breezeways. Each door is hard to open. They are thick storm doors made to keep the breeze out of the hallways which the rooms open into.

After the last door, I take the elevator down to the first floor. The hotel is two stories with breezeway connectors between each building.

The first building holds the breakfast room, the laundry area, the hotel lobby and rest rooms, and the exercise room. I enter the breakfast room.

The sun glares in through the floor to ceiling windows. I select a table in the far corner opposite from the sun.

Soon my little corner of breakfast space is filled with coffee, orange juice, oatmeal, an apple and a fresh hot waffle. I also have a pastry on a small plate and a couple of napkins.

I look around for a discarded newspaper. I saw no machines outside the lobby.

Newspapers had drifted away into the internet kind of like letter writing and telephone calls. Real connections with real people, I think, yet I'd never taken the time to write to Melody. Whether or not I had her letters, I knew I could've written her or called her.  Even when her Mom wouldn't tell me her address or her phone number, I could've tried and probably could've found someone else to tell me.  Or I could've hopped in the car and taken a drive.

I swallow the last bite of my oatmeal and the rest of my I could've thoughts and drain down the juice and coffee.  I wanted my stomach to be full for the day and it was.

I'm just an old man playing golf, I say to the guy in charge of the first golf and driving course I'd ever been to at the coast.  Just like on TV, just like in the pictures there was dark green lush grass, ponds filled with crystal blue water, sandbars made of pure golden sand, palm trees high with large green leaves moving about in the breeze.  It was an awesome sight!

I set my sights on the targets at the end of the range.  I miss every ball hitting a sclaff on each one.  I'm in pursuit of my unseen target hole way down the drive several hundred yards away, but I make no progress.  Managing RGC and being a Golf Pro were two different things.  As the Manager, I'd never found the time to play golf anymore.

A young man drops another bucket of balls at my feet.  He hollers "Good luck!" and moves on to the next golfer standing in the partition next to me.

I continue to hit bad drives, bad golf shots.  My wee white ball doesn't move at the thud of my golf club striking the ground behind the ball.  I dub, slice, hook, top, pull, push, sky, shank, and sclaff each shot.  I cannot get a good shot in, I think to myself.

I lean the club against the partition and stand up.  My back cracks a little.  I wipe my brow.  It was getting close to noon.

The young man comes at me with another bucket, but I wave him off.  I hand him a few dollars and say "I think it's time for me to call it quits."

He nods and says "Okay, old timer.  Save some for you tomorrow."

I mutter "thanks" and don't continue saying out loud what else I'm thinking.  I say to myself "It really is time for you to call it quits, old timer."

## Chapter Eleven

The little fridge doesn't hold as much as I thought. I sigh as I unload my few groceries and try placing them in different positions so everything will fit in the small space. I have milk, juice, iced tea, cheese, bread, and bottled water. I take what won't fit of the bottled water and put in on the floor in the closet space.

I place a large plastic container on top of the bottled water, and put my other groceries there. Crackers, peanut butter, paper plates, plastic utensils, paper cups, napkins, cereal bars, a bag of low sodium chips, and a bag of walnuts. I leave the bananas and apples out on the counter. I had enough to get by for lunch.

I flip on the TV and make a lunch of two peanut butter sandwiches, chips, an apple and a cup of Iced tea. I sit back on the bed to eat.

I try to keep the crumbs off me and the bed since the mMaid service had made everything up. I go back and forth on channels for a while watching the news, the weather and finally settling on the golf channel. I had really let my game go, I think. I finish the rest of my lunch and just listen to the ocean. Except for the ocean there was no noise at all.

Parking is not crowded at the Sunset Beach pier. I drove over the long bridge across the sound from Ocean Isle beach then down the road a bit and over another bridge to Sunset Beach. Sunset Beach to me was all straight rows of roads.

I drove to the end of the road where I'd been told was the best place to watch the sunsets, but there were only a few parking spaces. I could've parked in the street, but I might've gotten a ticket or been towed.

I ask a few people walking back from the beach about parking. Someone yells, park at the pier.

I drive the straight road back down and park at the end of the long sandy parking lot. There are huge signs everywhere about going into the pier to pay $8 to park since it's after a certain time of day.

I grab my hat, my camera, my jacket and lock the car. I stuff my little flip phone in my pocket. I wasn't sure if I had service or could really use the thing.

I knew my not being savvy and hip and up on smart phones and social media (and using words like savvy and hip) made me less desirable at RGC. They wanted Miss Young Thing to bring them into the new world of social media. Like social media would get people out to play golf in the little old town of Rionel.

I dismiss Rionel from my mind, and push the glass doors into the pier. The guy behind the desk is as gray and old looking as me. He's wearing a black tank top, has long gray hair curled behind him in a ponytail. His skin is a leathery brown and dark from the sun. He nods. I nod.

"Hey, I need to pay to park."

"Why, you going fishing at this hour?"

"Nah, nah." I shake my head. "Gotta friend. A girl. Well a woman now and she told me about this mail-."

"'Nuff said. The mailbox." He turns his back to me and holds is hand in the air and points. "You go thataway bout two miles down the beach. You think you won't see the thing, but it's there. Past the sand dunes."

He turns back around at me and grins. "Gotta admire your spunk, partner." He bends over and pulls something out from under the counter. He slams it on top. "Here you better take this."

I reach over and grab a black metal flashlight. "Thanks. What about the parking?"

He shakes his head. "On the house, man."

I nod. He nods. I head out the door.


I haven't walked on the beach in a long time. Maybe the last time I did it was during my senior year in high school, the senior trip to the beach. I had never been to Sunset Beach.

There aren't too many people on the beach. There are a few. Some are building sandcastles. A kid tries to fly a kite. Several are power walking. Some are taking pictures.

A couple of boats are moored further out in the ocean. I think they are fishing trawlers based on their design.

I can't see that far in the ocean. I can't see that far up the beach.

I walk slow and stop every few minutes to watch the waves rolling. I nod to every person I pass. After a while, I'm the only one headed south. Everyone else is heading towards the pier, not away from it like me.

I check my watch. I'd been walking thirty minutes. I stand still in the sand and let the orange yellow glow of the sunset wash over me.

I check my pockets. I had a pocket knife, a flashlight, and a pack of gum. I take out a piece and start chewing easy so I don't mess up my dental work.

A couple of ladies my age are walking up the beach. I nod and walk close to them.

"Excuse me. Have you heard of the mailbox? I'm trying to find it, but I'm not sure if I'm looking in the right place."

They stop and smile. One is shorter than the other. The short one is tan with long brown hair. The tall one is pale with a short blonde haircut.

The short one speaks first "Yeah, oh it's a bit of ways on down the beach, almost to the end, you know. Keep going past all the sand dunes. There's no marker like the guidebooks say, but there is a bench right near it. Just keep walking, you'll find it. It's a bit of a ways, though."

Before I can get out a thank you, the ladies turn around and continue their power walk on down the beach. I sigh and continue trudging forward. I should turn around. I should try this tomorrow. But I didn't want to wait any longer.

I try counting in my head, singing, reciting poetry, reciting famous quotes. I savor the entire sunset. A sunset on Sunset Beach is truly one of the most spectacular sights.

Every once in a while, I gaze away from the sunset at the trawlers. Their lights were my only guide. I turn back and the pier's lights looked tiny in the distance. I'd lost track of how far I walked. I was now the only person on the beach and it was almost dark.

I ignore the dark and keep walking. I press on churning the sand underneath my shoes. I stop for a moment and take them off pressing my toes deep into the cool sand.

Walking on sand is like being on a soft plush carpet only it's squishy and a little gritty feeling. I can walk a little faster with my shoes in my hand.

I grip my toes, use the trawler lights for bearings and start counting sand dunes. Every time I thought I had passed the last dune, there was another one and then another one.

I see black shadows everywhere coming out from the dunes and over them. The only noise comes from the ocean. It's just me and the waves, the sand, the dunes, and the engulfing darkness.

I pass more and more darkened sand dunes. I start to think that it was all a joke, that the mailbox didn't really exist, and that the ladies I talked to early about how to find it had made it all up not wanting to disappoint me. No one wanted to admit they'd walked all that way to find nothing.

I keep trudging, I keep moving, I keep looking for nothing and then I see the end of the dunes, the brown wooden bench, and next to it … the mailbox.

## Chapter Twelve

The mailbox is a real mailbox.  It even has a red metal flag.  It's held up by a wooden pole buried deep in the sand and a platform.  The pole and platform is white with graffiti of names and messages written all up and down and across and sideways.  Where ever there was space, there was a name or a message.

I try to read a few as I catch my breath.  I step towards the bench and plop down.

The mailbox was set back from the last dunes sort of in an alcove of sand.  The wind swirled up and in and over the hidden spot.

I listen to the wind, the waves, and watch the glow of the fishing boat lights way out in the blackness.  I pull my flashlight from my pocket.  Its glow is a round orb of bright white light a speck only in the darkness.

I shine it towards the mailbox.  I wanted to run to the box, tear it open and find something just for me.  I wasn't sure.  I couldn't be sure.  I could've gone to the real post office, or used the yellow pages but I wanted to see for myself if it would possibly be true.  I suck in air and exhale and check my pulse.  I was not used to walking that far that fast.  I stare at the box.  It was a shiny white.  I wondered how it was, looked so clean.  Maybe the rain.  Maybe a caretaker.  Or maybe something above and beyond both of those things.

I clear my thoughts of earth, of sand, wind, fishing boats and darkness. I move forward. I take a deep breath. I open the box.

I gawk at the box's innards for maybe twenty or thirty seconds before I shut my mouth again. The small mailbox was crammed with letters and journals. There was a small plastic box of pennies from heaven inside it, too.

I thumb through the letters, I page through the journals. Inside the letters, the journals were people's innermost thoughts to those they had lost or loved and lost or lost touch with or who were really and truly lost or even lost forever.

The letters were on notebook paper, scraps of paper, construction paper, pretty stationery, or notecards. All were hand written in cursive, blocks, print, or a mixture of both. I see names and drawings and photos taped to the writings. There are none for me. There is nothing with my name, Ernie, on it.

I shuffle through the writings one more time. I am careful to put everything back as I found it.

The last thing I put back is the plastic box of pennies. I sigh and pull off the lid. "Might as well take one of these and leave it somewhere." I knew that pennies from heaven were sometimes found after losing a loved one. I pulled a dull Lincoln wheat penny out from 1947 turning it over in my hands. I put it in my pocket.

I set down the box and start to put the lid back on but stop. Inside a corner underneath a pile of pennies, I see it, I see my name sticking up from the pennies. "Oh Melody. You put this here."

I laugh, I smile, I unfold the piece of paper. I return the pennies back to the mailbox and shut it closed.

I move over to the bench, sit down and read. It's her hand writing all right except shakier and not as neat. There was no date. Just a short quick note.

Dearest Ernie,


I see you made it. You walked all the way from the Sunset Pier to the mailbox. Have you ever walked this far? Is this your first time walking on the beach since high school?

I knew you'd come here, one day. Did you enjoy the walk? Isn't Sunset Beach beautiful? I hope you plan to stay and do something different. RGC will be fine without you, I promise!

What've I been up to? Why did I write you this letter?

I've had a great career at the museum. I've become a very good fisherman or fisherwoman. It's what I've been doing all these years for relaxation, and for supper!

I bet I'm making you hungry.  Well depending on the time of

year, and of course what year it is, you'll find me at the pier at Ocean

Isle.  I'll be fishing!

Yours Truly,

Melody


PS  Watch out for the sand crabs on the way back if you're out here at

dark.


I fold the letter and place it in my pocket.  I shake my head and smile.  I

whisper "Melody."

## Chapter Thirteen

The walk back in the dark on the beach on the sand with the ocean waves lapping and the only light flickering from the two trawlers way out in the water and the distant ones from the pier is not easy, but I make a good pace of it. I turn my flashlight on when the waves lap close. I turn it off when there's a wider span of sand so I can save the light just in case.

As I get closer to the pier, I don't need the light. I see groups of people with buckets and flashlights. They chase after sand crabs.

I don't chase the sand crabs. I jump and try to move to the side to stay out of their way. Some of the crabs are tiny. Some are quite large. Whatever their size, I don't want to get bitten.

I watch some teenagers run with buckets and lights and gather up a group of them. Another group of kids, hoses off under the outdoor showers by the pier. I figure they were on the sand all day, or in the ocean.

I have had a big dose of the ocean, the most I'd had in many years. I wait my turn and hose off my feet and sandals.

The sand feels good underneath my toes. I use the restroom in the parking lot and head for my car.

I sit for a minute and re-read the letter. I smile. I think about it all the way back to the hotel.

I lay it out on the desk, put my wet shoes up to dry and pull my pajamas from the drawer.  I turn on the TV and lie down asleep almost as soon as my head hits the pillow.

## Chapter Fourteen

The orange ball of sun wakes me up with a smile. I shave, shower, dress and wolf down my complimentary apple and oatmeal breakfast. I have a bowl full of plain grits too along with coffee, apple juice and a cup of water.

I throw away my paper plates, cups, bowls, and napkins and go outside by the outdoor pool and Tiki Bar taking the boardwalk onto the beach. I walk out to the ocean and savor the smells, the sounds, the view of seagulls, kids running and playing and the surf. I continue on down the beach until I reach a public access stairway to a public parking lot.

I walk up the stairs, into the lot, and head on into the few blocks that made up the shopping and store area of Ocean Isle. I step inside a small gift shop and wander around until I find what I'm looking for: a small bouquet of large yellow and orange sunflowers, Melody's favorite I remember her Mom once said when a customer gave some to her at the Grill.

I ask the clerk to tie up the plastic around the flower with a neat yellow ribbon and bow. I hold it up in the light. I say "Wonder what's missing?"

The lady smiles and hands me a card to attach to the bouquet. I grin. I take the pen she holds out and jot a quick note: "Melody, I know it's taken all these years to write back to you, but here's my note. I have thought of no one but you all these years. Let's spend the time we have left together. Yours Truly, Ernie."

I clutch the flowers to my chest and bounce out of the store. I have no address, but I do know where the museum is – it's the only one in Ocean Isle.

Just inside the museum at a small podium at the entrance, a lady with a coastal accent peers at me through reading glasses. She wears a tight curly hairdo piled on top of her head. She hands out scavenger hunt maps to kids or to parents with kids as she explains why the museum entrance tickets cost what they do (privately funded, no government or matching funds) and why it's a good idea to become a member (can go to sister museums for free, get discounts in the gift shops). She answers my question about where to find Melody in almost the same breath as she answers the membership benefits and ticket price questions, "Oh you're one of those looking for our Melody, are you, she was quite well known from her work her at the museum and the fishing, well now just go to the pier she's easy enough to find up 'bout halfway on the left."

I repeat "about hallway up the pier on the left" to myself, smile and nod and bounce back out of the store. I tumble across the parking lot and stop for a moment outside of a coffee shop. Along the walls, there are paper boxes lined up in rows. The boxes are selling every kind of newspaper imaginable. Across from it, is a gift and surf shop with piles of surfboards, boogie boards and floats stacked outside.

The store and the coffee shop are not far from the pier, only a couple of blocks.  I enter the pier through the shaved ice store and walk up to the counter.  The guy behind it wears a smile, a sweat stained white t-shirt, and baggy shorts with holes in them.  His hair is greased back in a comb over.

"It's a dollar to walk the pier.  Two dollars if you gonna throw them flowers over in the water or something."

I fish out a dollar from my pocket. "Just walking the pier, I promise."

"Ah, one of those I see."

He takes my dollar and points to the double glass doors.  I take a deep breath and push them open and step out onto the pier.

## Chapter Fifteen

I walk out on the pier and a blast of wind hits my face. I push forward and stare at the sun.

Ahead I could see the silhouettes of fisherman. There were four already out on the pier.

I stop and talk to the first fisherman I see. He is packing up his gear.

"No luck today?"

He grins. Shakes his head. "Too muddy down there. He points to the ocean. The rains, the tides, fish don't like all that mud. Only caught a handful." He points to a white bucket beside him on the pier.

I glance in the bucket. A few small fish were swimming around in some fresh water.

"I'll wait. Try again tomorrow."

I nod and keep on walking down the pier. I pass a couple of sinks for washing and cutting up fish as they were caught, weathered wooden benches for fishermen or anyone walking the pier, metal round pole slots for fishing poles, and light poles.

I stop by a light pole and look over the side. I was way over the cold midnight dark blue rolling waves. I look down at the beach and back at the houses, hotels, and people walking, throwing balls, or strewn about on the beach making sand castles, swimming in the waves, walking their dogs, a flurry of early morning sunny weather beach activities.

I start walking again and stop when I come to more fishermen. These two tall dark headed guys were pals or brothers finishing each other's sentences when I asked them questions.

"What you catching?"

"Small ones. Bit of--."

"Mid-size ones too. Them good at taking the--."

"Bait. But we're low on it and don't want to--."

"Waste it. Too pricey to buy at the pier."

I smile and say "The pier. Fishing. I don't know much about fishing or bait. I was looking for someone."

They punch each other in the shoulders and grin back "Yeah, we know. You got them flowers."

I stare out over the end of the pier into the water. It was deep, churning, a dark green and midnight blue this far out.

"Hey man. Try back at the first of the pier. You walked right past. Must've been off looking at the water in a water fog like you're now. You'll find what you're looking for. You're one of them from the mailbox on Sunset, right? You're looking for her, right?"

I'm not sure which one said what or what they meant.  I turn around, smile and nod, clutch my flowers and start walking.

Behind me one of the men yells, "On the right, on the right."

**Chapter Sixteen**

I keep walking on the pier. I yell back a "thank you." I'm not sure if the guys heard me or not.

I stop at the mid-point of the pier and face the sky. The seagulls form a perfect V shape and come towards me flying overhead. "Maybe the seagulls are having better luck with the fish," I mumble.

I turn to the center of the pier. Up above in the skyline, I see the Ocean Isle water tower. I can see the bright blue building that housed the museum where Melody worked. I watch the water. The waves. I let the sound of the ocean surround me.

The waves continue to churn. A couple of surfers emerge from underneath the pier. They are wearing wet suits in black and bright blue, red, yellow, orange or green colors.

Their surfboards are even brighter colors of yellow, orange, purple, pink with stripes, designs, swirls, lines, circles. A group of four or five circles swim in a row beside each other. They head out into the ocean and stay in the same line waiting for a wave to break.

I watch the surfers for a few more minutes. My gaze drifts to the edge of the pier, near where my new friends said I should look.

I see no one. I watch the door to the bait, game room and snack bar shop at the entrance to the pier. I see a face, but it soon disappears.

I keep walking and look to the right. I walk for hours, for miles, for days, for decades – at least it seems that way.

I kick my shoes on the rough wood planks as a leaf or something falls on one of them. I kick hard and then stop kicking when I determine what has fallen on my shoe – a rose petal.

A trail of rose petals leads to the right and stops by one of the fishing pole stands and benches. I found her. I had found Melody.

I step over to the side and grasp the banister. I stare down at the plague and read it three or four times before I drop the flowers, before the tears slide down my cheeks, before I sob into my hands and ask myself why I had waited so long, too long. I was too late. You waited for me. I found you. I was too late.

**The Plaque:**
      "Here lies Melody's favorite fishing spot.
      She's a catching one up in Heaven just for you!"

## The End:  On the Ocean Isle Pier

There you are
it's really you
I found you
I found you
on the pier
like everyone said
you always fished
on the pier
this was your
favorite fishing spot
over the sides
in the ocean
the muddy ocean
catching bass, flounder
you cooked it
you sold it
fishing supported you
your last letter
was to me
here you are
I step back
I'm talking to
no one except
myself I am
alone I step
back and stare
at the gold
plague with your
name your beautiful
name the gold
faded the name
a bit rusted
but the plague
attached to the
pier where you
fished and waited
waited for me
here I am

I found you
except you are
gone but at
least I know
that on this
pier on this
spot at one
time you were
here.


*Ocean Isle Beach Pier - April 17, 2017*

# About the Author
## L.B. Sedlacek

LB Sedlacek is a poet, author, editor, poem critic and publisher. She has had poetry and short fiction published in numerous poetry magazines, journals and zines. Her poetry and short fiction have won several awards. She co-hosted ESC! Magazine's podcast for the small press, "Coffee House to Go" with Michael Potter. She also served as a Poetry Editor for "ESC! Magazine." She is the Publisher of "The Poetry Market Ezine" a free poetry resource newsletter just for poets. She also teaches poetry locally to elementary and middle school kids. Her latest chapbook is "Words and Bones" published by Finishing Line Press. In her free time, LB enjoys reading, traveling, and swimming. *www.lbsedlacek.com*

## ALSO BY LB SEDLACEK:

### POETRY
Alexandra's Wreck (Kitty Litter Press)
Constellate (GoatsonMars Press)
Hemlock Suicides Planned by Well Dressed Men in Suits (Assume Nothing Press)
Hey Astro! (GoatsonMars Press)
Infra Dig (It's a Chemical Life) (GoatsonMars Press)
Mars or Bust (GoatsOnMars Press)
Poetry in LA – Only in LA (LA Poems) (GoatsonMars Press)
The Cat & The *Carroll A. Deering* and Other North Carolina Poems (Pop Poets
    Press)
Spy Techniques (Four2Three Press)
The Adventures of Stick People on Cars (Alien Buddha Press)
The Architect of French Fries (Presa Press)
Twisting (Four2Three Press)
Words and Bones (Finishing Line Press)

### FICTION
The E.P. Hunting Club – Book One "The Poem Code" ISBN 978-1-365-01734-6
The E.P. Hunting Club – Book Two "Redshift"
The Glass River
Traveling with Fish

### NON-FICTION
Life after Wreck – Memoir (Four2Three Press) ISBN 978-1-329-91674-6
The Catnip Gene – non-fiction E-book (Four2Three Press)

# THE MAILBOX OF THE KINDRED SPIRIT
## By LB Sedlacek

These are the pennies from Heaven we left in the mailbox in April 2017 in memory of my Dad who's always sending us pennies from Heaven. When we returned to the mailbox in 2018, they were all gone! It's still a special place to visit, this mailbox near the end of the island with the marsh on one side, the ocean on the other … very serene.

Made in the USA
Columbia, SC
21 December 2019